Bobby's Big Bear Hunt

by Gwendolyn Hooks

illustrated by Alessia Girasole

RED
CHAIR
•PRESS•

Bobby loves to fish.
But not today.

2

"The fish aren't biting," says Bobby.
"I'm not having fun."
His sister, Lizzie, reels in a big fish.
She grins at him.

"That's not funny," says Bobby.
"I'm going on a bear hunt."

4

Bobby stomps off down the trail.
"Wait," yells Lizzie.
"Dad says for us to stay together."

"I'll find the biggest bear in the woods," Bobby says. "I'm not afraid!"

Bobby walks and walks.
But soon the trail disappears.

Bobby stops. He looks up at the tall trees.
He hears a screech from the treetops.
Something flaps and dives near him.

Something dives into a hole.
Something else splashes into the creek.
Something big moves in the bushes.

Bobby looks around him.
"Where is the trail?" he wonders.
Grrr!

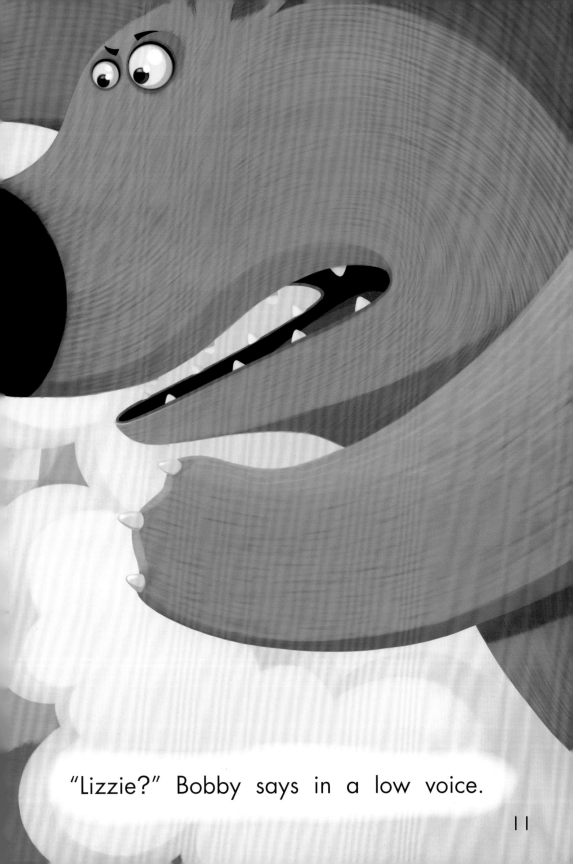

"Lizzie?" Bobby says in a low voice.

GRRRR!
"LIZZIE!" Bobby yells in a loud voice. He starts to run.

"It's just me," says Lizzie.
She giggles and laughs.
"That's not funny!" says Bobby.

"Next time, we stay together," says Lizzie.
"Don't worry," Bobby says. "I'll stay as
close to you as the bugs in your hair!"

"Today is fun after all."

Big Question: Why is it important to use a Buddy System? What might have happened to Bobby if Lizzie had not followed him?

Big Words:

disappear: to no longer be in view

stomp: to walk with hard, loud steps

screech: a high pitched cry

splash: the sound water makes when something enters suddenly